PUFFIN BOOKS

TOO COOL FOR SCHOOL, HAMMY THE WONDER HAMSTER!

Hamilton was still so sleepy that, for the moment, he had forgotten all about the Kitty. He peeped out from the nest box and saw Bethany smiling down at him.

'Hello, Hamilton!' she said. 'You look very sleepy in –' Then she stopped and went to the door. 'Sorry, Mum, what did you say?'

For a minute, Bethany stood at the bedroom door while Mum said something that Hamilton couldn't hear. She came back with a bang of the door that made the cage tremble.

'Kitty's coming!' she exclaimed. 'Why do we have to have Kitty! She's a *monster*!'

Hamilton bolted backwards into the box and hid. Not only a cat, but a monster cat! How much worse could it get?

Have you read all of Hammy's adventures?

POPPY HARRIS

TOO COOL FOR SCHOOL, HAMMY THE WONDER HAMSTER!

PUFFIN

PUFFIN BOOKS

Published by the Penguin Group
Penguin Books Ltd, 80 Strand, London WC2R ORL, England
Penguin Group (USA) Inc., 375 Hudson Street, New York, New York 10014, USA
Penguin Group (Canada), 90 Eglinton Avenue East, Suite 700, Toronto, Ontario, Canada M4P 2Y3
(a division of Pearson Penguin Canada Inc.)
Penguin Ireland, 25 St Stephen's Green, Dublin 2, Ireland (a division of Penguin Books Ltd)
Penguin Group (Australia), 250 Camberwell Road, Camberwell, Victoria 3124, Australia
(a division of Pearson Australia Group Pty Ltd)
Penguin Books India Pvt Ltd, 11 Community Centre, Panchsheel Park, New Delhi – 110 017, India
Penguin Group (NZ), 67 Apollo Drive, Rosedale, North Shore 0632, New Zealand
(a division of Pearson New Zealand Ltd)
Penguin Books (South Africa) (Pty) Ltd, 24 Sturdee Avenue, Rosebank, Johannesburg 2196, South Africa

Penguin Books Ltd, Registered Offices: 80 Strand, London WC2R ORL, England

puffinbooks.com

First published 2010
1

Text copyright © Poppy Harris, 2010
Illustrations copyright © Dan Bramall, 2010
All rights reserved

The moral right of the author and illustrator has been asserted

Set in 13.75/20.5pt Bembo
Typeset by Palimpsest Book Production Limited, Grangemouth, Stirlingshire
Made and printed in England by Clays Ltd, St Ives plc

British Library Cataloguing in Publication Data
A CIP catalogue record for this book is available from the British Library

ISBN: 978-0-141-32487-6

www.greenpenguin.co.uk

Mixed Sources
Product group from well-managed
forests and other controlled sources
www.fsc.org Cert no. SA-COC-1592
© 1996 Forest Stewardship Council

Penguin Books is committed to a sustainable future
for our business, our readers and our planet.
The book in your hands is made from paper
certified by the Forest Stewardship Council.

For Thomas Priestley

chapter 1

It was a busy, rushing-about Monday morning
in Bethany's house. Mum was yelling upstairs to
Bethany that her friend Chloe was waiting for
her while Bethany was still throwing books,
pens and pencils into her school bag. Sam was
running downstairs and shouting, 'I'm getting
my trombone today! I'm getting my trombone!'

Hamilton, Bethany's hamster, was sitting on
Bethany's bed reading a book about the Battle
of Hastings. It was all so exciting that at first he
hardly noticed what Sam was saying. At last he

looked up, listened carefully with his head on one side, then looked for Bethany's mobile phone. Bethany always left it where he could reach it in case he needed to tell or ask her anything.

Sam's shout had puzzled Hamilton. He knew the names of all the bones in hamsters, humans and most other animals, from the skull to the tiny little phalanges in the toes, but he'd never heard of a trom-bone. Was it another word for a toe bone, or a vertebra? Or was 'trom' a word for something else, like an arm, a rib, or a shoulder? Did anyone get a fractured trombone at the Battle of Hastings?

Bethany heard the faint click of his claws on the keypad and looked up from her packing to see what he was telling her, and when Hamilton had finished the message, he pushed the phone towards her. She hoped it was something simple. She was running a bit late this morning and should really be on her way to school by now.

'What's a "trom-bone"?' she read out loud, pushing her hair back. She closed the book about the Battle of Hastings and put it into her bag. 'Ah! You mean a 'trombone'.

That's exactly what I said! thought Hamilton. But he listened to Bethany's explanation as he always liked learning new things.

'It's a musical instrument,' Bethany revealed. 'It's very big and made of brass, and *very* loud – and it makes a horrible noise, or it certainly will when Sam tries to play it.'

Hamilton still sat with his head tipped to one side. He wanted to know more, but Bethany didn't have time this morning to explain all about trombones.

'It makes oompah music,' she finished cryptically. 'See you later. Be good.'

Bethany picked him up, kissed him and put

him back in his cage as Mum shouted for her again. 'Bethany! NOW!'

'I'm coming!' she called. 'Hi, Chloe!' And she ran down the stairs and out of the house.

Dad was already at work, and Mum (who was a dressmaker and sometimes worked at home) soon went out to visit a customer. Hamilton was alone in the house, longing to know more about trombones and knowing exactly how to find out about them. All he needed was a computer. Hamilton knew a lot about computers, but what he didn't know was where all his knowledge came from.

The secret – which not even he knew – was that, lodged in Hamilton's cheek pouch was a very tiny microchip, so small that it was only a micro*speck*. It was this that gave him all his most un-hamster-like intelligence. It made

Hamilton able to read, think, calculate, speak hundreds of languages (including Rabbit, which came in useful) and to know lots about computers.

Hamilton had accidentally and unknowingly eaten the microspeck, which had been made by a very clever young scientist called Tim Taverner. And Tim was trying to get it back. Tim, who worked at the university, had already made a remote-control tracking device to help him find the hamster with his precious microspeck. He had even found out where Bethany lived, but so far, he'd never quite managed to get hold of Hamilton. Neither Hamilton nor Bethany knew anything about him.

As soon as the house was empty Hamilton let himself out of his cage (or his 'apartment', as he liked to think of it), scrambled down the stairs and ran to the dining room, where the computer was kept.

He was distracted by the sight of a newspaper lying over the back of a chair. Hamilton loved newspapers. He very much wanted to stop, read it and do all the puzzles, but with a great effort he ran past it. He had to get on to the Internet as soon as he could because he couldn't risk Mum coming home and finding him at the computer. His great intelligence was a secret between Bethany and himself.

Bother! thought Hamilton as he looked up at the desk. Last time he'd been in there, somebody had left a pile of books on the floor, just right for climbing up to the desk. Why had they been tidied away? Getting up to the computer wasn't going to be so easy now. He'd have to work out a route.

The leg of the swivel chair looked too smooth to run up, but Hamilton tried it all the same. After he had fallen off for the third time he decided that, yes, it *was* too difficult (although it had been great fun trying). He sat back to take a good look at the possible new ways up.

The dining room was also the room Mum used for sewing. In the corner stood a small white chest of drawers in which she kept all sorts of needlework things – beads, brocade, buckles, buttons, pins, needles, zips and seven different kinds of elastic. There were five drawers, each with a small metal handle. It would be a long stretch or a bit of a jump, but Hamilton thought he might be able to use it as a ladder. It was worth a try. He sprang on to the lowest handle, wobbled a bit until he got his balance, and with a stretch and a jump, managed to scramble on to the next one. By the time he had reached the top, Hamilton had decided it was so easy that he jumped all the way down the drawer handles and back up again just for fun before climbing on to the top of the sewing table. From there, one good leap took him on to the computer desk.

He clicked on the search engine. Spelling out 'trombone' (which he'd now worked out was all one word) was a bit difficult because it was hard to tap on the right keys without standing on the wrong ones at the same time, so he'd typed in 'grimbone', 'tronbike' and 't4ib9n3' before he had the idea of picking up a pencil in both paws and tapping the keys with that. Suddenly, a picture of a huge and impressive brass instrument appeared on the page. So *that* was a trombone! Amazing!

In no time at all, Hammy learnt a great deal about trombones, and it was all very exciting. He loved the size and shape and shine of them, and listening on the computer to the deep, confident noise they made.

'. . . *often played by oompah bands* . . .' he also read. Bethany had said something about oompah. He'd better find out what an oompah band was. A few more clicks of the mouse and up came a picture of some very happy men with big moustaches, hats, short leather trousers and trombones. *Oompah men!* thought Hamilton, and pressed Play.

One-two-three, one-two-three, oompah-pah, oompah-pah . . . It was happy and rhythmical and Hamilton loved it. It made him sway from side to side, swinging his paws, and soon he was waltzing across the desk – *one-two-three, one-two-three!* When the music stopped he started it again and went on dancing until a click from somewhere near the front door made him jump.

Help! He'd been enjoying the music so much, he'd forgotten to be careful! Was Mum arriving home? What would she think if she found him on the desk, playing trombone music on the computer? Only Bethany knew how clever Hamilton was. But to Hamilton's relief, nothing happened. The door didn't open and Hamilton realized that the click had only been the sound of the letterbox opening and shutting. He returned the computer to the screensaver (in case Mum really did come home), ran down the sewing-box ladder and scampered to the door to pick up the printed yellow paper lying on the mat. He knew it hadn't been delivered by the postman because it had no envelope and wasn't stamped. He tasted it, didn't like it, and turned it over to read.

PEXPERTS

THE PET EXPERTS

EXPERT ADVICE FOR PET OWNERS

AT PEXPERTS, WE DEAL WITH ALL FORMS OF

ANIMAL BEHAVIOUR. NO PROBLEM IS TOO

STRANGE FOR US. FROM DOPEY DOGS TO

MAD MICE, WE CAN HELP. FOR SNAKES'
SHAKES, DIZZY LIZARDS AND HABITS OF
RABBITS, PEXPERTS ARE EXPERTS. IF YOUR
PET IS SAD, STROPPY, BAD, BORED OR
BONKERS, CALL US. WE SPECIALIZE IN
RODENTS, ESPECIALLY HAMSTERS.
PHONE FOR A FREE VISIT.

At the bottom of the page was a mobile phone
number. Hamilton rushed up the stairs,
scrabbling for clawholds on the carpet,
and found Bethany's phone. PEXPERTS
sounded wonderful to him. They might
even help him to talk, or at least teach him
games to play. It was all very exciting. He
tapped a text into the phone to the Pexperts
number: PLS CALL AT 33 TUMBLERS CRESCENT,
SPINHILL.

★

In his lab at the university, Tim Taverner picked up the special mobile he had bought just for these calls and smiled to himself as he read the message. This was exactly what he had hoped for.

chapter 2

Having sent the text message, Hamilton ran downstairs again. There might be time for a quick look at that newspaper while the family were still out. He'd have to listen for Mum coming home, but he was pretty sure he could be up the stairs and back into his cage before she saw him. He sat on the paper washing his whiskers while he read all about the weather in Japan and what the government was doing. Then he burrowed into the pages and found the Sudoku and the crossword. Puzzles were among his favourite things. He had worked out the Sudoku in his head and was trying the crossword when the telephone rang.

'Hello,' said the voice of Bethany's mum on the phone, 'this is Angela. Sorry, there's nobody who can take your call just now. If you want to leave a message, please speak after the tone.'

The first time this had happened, Hamilton had been most confused. Mum hadn't been in the house, but he could still hear her voice. He had been very impressed, though, after Bethany had explained about voice messages. It was yet more information for Hamilton to store up delightedly.

'Hello, Angela, it's Sally here,' answered another woman's voice. 'Sorry, but can you help me out today? I've got an appointment in town this afternoon and I can't take Kitty with me. Can I leave her with you? I'll pick her up from school and drop her at your house. I should only be about an hour – is that OK? I've just tried your mobile, but you must have left it switched off. Kitty loves coming to you. See you soon – thanks!'

The machine clicked again. Hamilton waited to see if it did anything else, but nothing happened.

He was really very keen to have one more go with the computer, and he wasn't sure what the woman on the phone had meant by 'Kitty'. The computer would help him to find out. He ran back up the sewing box, leapt to the keyboard, and entered 'Kitty' in the search engine.

To his horror, a cat loomed at him from the screen. He clicked again and saw another cat, and then another! He jumped back. He knew they were only pictures of cats, but they were very close and frighteningly big, and had sprung out at him so quickly that it was unfair. *Computers shouldn't be allowed to shock you like that*, thought Hamilton. It was very annoying.

He read the words on the screen and didn't feel any better. According to this site, a kitty was a cat! He had met a cat once before and didn't want to meet any more. It had been an enormous animal with terrible claws and far too many sharp teeth – and it wanted fresh hamster for supper and might have had it too, if Bethany hadn't turned up when she did. He still felt shaky just thinking about it.

So, who was Sally and why did she want to leave a cat here? It was all very well saying that it would only be for about an hour. For Hamilton, even a minute with a cat would be a minute too long.

He needed to get out of the way quickly before the Kitty arrived. He ran upstairs, climbed into his cage, fastened the door firmly behind him and pulled paper and sawdust into his nest box. Having made the nest as big as possible, he made himself as small as possible, and snuggled down.

The nest was extremely comfortable, and it had been a busy morning for Hamilton. He was soon asleep and only woke up when the door banged and Bethany's school bag thudded on to the floor.

Hamilton was still so sleepy that, for the moment, he had forgotten all about the Kitty. He peeped out from the nest box and saw Bethany smiling down at him.

'Hello, Hamilton!' she said. 'You look very cosy in –' Then she stopped and went to the door. 'Sorry, Mum, what did you say?'

For a minute, Bethany stood at the bedroom door while Mum said something that Hamilton couldn't hear. She came back with a bang of the door that made the cage tremble.

'Kitty's coming!' she exclaimed. 'Why do we have to have Kitty! She's a *monster*!'

Hamilton bolted backwards into the box and hid. Not only a cat, but a monster cat! How much worse could it get?

chapter 3

Deep in the nest, Hamilton listened hard for
any sound that could warn him of the approach
of the Kitty. A monster cat would have a
monstrous mew, surely, and a purr like the
roaring of an engine. Sure enough, there were
alarming noises coming from Sam's bedroom
– very alarming noises – but they didn't sound
a bit like a cat. He heard a long, miserable
groan. There was a pause, a creak, a squeak, a
hoot and, at last, silence.

That was better. Whatever had been making that noise, it didn't sound happy.

Then the silence was broken by an enormous roar like the bellowing of a dinosaur with its foot stuck in the swamp. Only a Kitty Monster could make a noise like that! It must be the size of an elephant! Two elephants! He hoped it wasn't hungry!

Hamilton peeped out to see Bethany's face up close to his cage. She had sorted out her books and changed out of her school uniform and was looking a bit puzzled and disappointed. Hamilton knew that Bethany would be wondering why he wasn't ready to come out of his cage and play.

'Hamilton?' she said. 'You've been hiding in there ever since I came home. Are you all right?'

Hamilton glanced around the room to make sure he couldn't see anything that might be a

Monstrous Kitty, and scrambled out of the nest box to the bars of his cage. The dinosaur bellowed again and he dived into a corner.

'Oh, Hamilton, is that what frightened you?' she said. 'That's nothing to be afraid of. It's only Sam playing his trombone.'

Hamilton put his head on one side. Could that noise really be a trombone? It didn't sound half as good as the wonderful oompah music on the computer. He had really liked that.

'I know,' said Bethany. 'It's terrible. But his teacher said that all beginners make noises like that. It takes a long time before you can play a trombone without horrible sounds coming out of it – but never mind the trombone just now. I've got something important to tell you. My Auntie Sally phoned this morning. She's Mum's sister. She's bringing Kitty here today. I wish she wasn't, but she is, and Kitty is an absolute horror. Unfortunately, we have to put up with her now and again.'

Why? wondered Hamilton. The message on the answering machine had only said, 'Can I leave her with you?'. Maybe this monster cat was so dangerous that it had to be watched by a keeper at all times. If Kitty was a Monster Cat of Absolute Horror, why wasn't she kept in a cage? He was, and he was a harmless hamster. Hamilton would never hurt anyone (although when he came to think of it, he might nip someone who took away his food, his water bottle or his crossword – oh, and anyone who tried to hurt Bethany).

'I don't think Sam knows about Kitty coming,' said Bethany. 'He was making too much noise to hear Mum. I'd better go and warn him.'

Bethany crossed the landing. Soon, Sam was running noisily down the stairs.

'Don't let her near my trombone, either!' he shouted.

Bethany came back.

'Sam's gone to check that the shed door's locked, so Kitty can't get near Bobby the Bunny,' said Bethany. 'And the key has to go on a high shelf so she can't reach it. Mum and Dad are putting everything away in high places and I think I'd better do the same.'

Bethany gathered together her school books, her phone and some pretty things – necklaces and china animals – from her desk and the windowsill. While she climbed on to a chair to stack these things safely on the top shelf of her wardrobe, Hamilton let himself out of his cage and sat on the pillowcase, waiting for her to put him up there too. He wondered what Monstrous Kitty of the Absolute Horror would look like. At least if she couldn't reach the high shelves she couldn't be all that big –

certainly not as big as an elephant – but even ordinary cats were much bigger than he was. Really, Kitty Monsters shouldn't be allowed out. What if it came Monstering in and attacked Bethany? He'd have to bite it – he would do that for Bethany.

From Sam's room came a click, a thump and a bump. Hamilton stood up on his hind legs, ready to either fight or run away.

'It's all right, Hamilton,' said Bethany, climbing down. 'That's just Sam shutting his trombone in its case because he doesn't want Kitty anywhere near it. Now, I'll tell you what we're going to do with you. I'm taking you round to Chloe's house – all right? You can stay there until Kitty's gone.'

This sounded to Hamilton like a very sensible idea. Chloe was Bethany's best friend. She had a hamster of her own, Toffee, so she understood about hamsters. (Although she did insist on calling him 'Hammy', which he wasn't so impressed with.)

'I'd like to stay there with you,' said Bethany. 'But if Kitty goes raging round the house, she'll get into my room and wreck things, so I'd better be here. I need to keep her away from Sam too because he can't stand her.'

There were voices downstairs, then a car door banged. Bethany ran to look out of the window, and Hamilton saw a look of horror on her face.

'It's too late!' she whispered. 'Kitty's here!'

'I want to play in Bethany's room!' yelled a loud and piercing voice.

'I don't want her even to see you!' Bethany whispered urgently.

Hamilton gave the door catch on his cage an extra hard twist to make sure it was as tightly shut as possible before tunnelling into the safety of his nest box. As footsteps pounded up the stairs, Bethany threw her coat over the cage to hide it. The bedroom door was flung open.

Hamilton was worried, but he was also extremely curious about the Monstrous Kitty. He peeped out very cautiously and found a gap at one corner where the coat hadn't quite covered the bars of the cage. It looked like a good place for spying on the Kitty Monster without being seen.

But there was no cat, and certainly not an enormous one. In the doorway stood a small person with ribboned bunches of blonde hair. She wore a very pink sweater and trousers, and sparkly trainers. She jumped up and down twice and Hamilton, feeling the floor shake, crept backwards.

'Hello, Bethany!' shouted the Kitty. 'I've come to play! Let's get all the toys out! You're my very bestest cousin!'

With an enormous bounce, Kitty launched

herself on to Bethany's bed. The springs
creaked.

So she's not a monster cat, thought Hamilton.
She's just Bethany's little cousin. That can't be so
bad, can it?

chapter 4

'Let's get everything out!' shouted Kitty. 'Let's get *all* the toys out!'

'No, Kitty,' said Bethany firmly. 'You can only get out one thing at a time.'

'Paint, paint, paint!' shouted Kitty, bouncing with every word.

'Kitty, you've been told before about bouncing on the bed,' said Bethany.

Kitty bounced again.

Bethany folded her arms and stood still. She was used to her little cousin Kitty.

'Do you want to paint or don't you?' she asked calmly.

Kitty jumped down from the bed with a thud that made Hamilton flinch. 'Paint, paint, paint!' she said again.

Bethany remembered all too well what had happened last time Kitty had got her hands on, or rather in, the paint. There were still purple stains on the carpet, but Bethany had hidden them under a small fluffy rug between the bed and the wardrobe. 'You'll need an apron,' she said. 'And we'll do the painting in the bathroom.'

'But I like your bedroom best!' wailed Kitty. She grabbed at a handful of felt pens, but Bethany was too quick for her and snatched them away before she could draw on the walls.

'I want the pens!' screamed Kitty.

'Do you? I thought you wanted to paint,' said Bethany with great patience.

'Pe-he-hens!' whinged Kitty, trying to sound as if she were crying. She could make herself cry very easily, but Bethany was used to that and looked around for something to distract Kitty quickly, before she could damage anything. There was a kaleidoscope that Kitty sometimes liked to play with.

'Would you like to look in the kaleidoscope?' she suggested.

'Klidoscope, klidoscope, klidoscope, Bethany is a klidoscope!' sang Kitty, and climbed on the bed again. This time she lost her balance, wobbled, looked for something to hold on to, and grabbed the curtain. When the curtain came off the rail, even Kitty looked subdued.

'Get down off the bed, Kitty,' ordered Bethany. Normally, Kitty would have refused, but just for a few seconds, she was worried that she might really be in trouble, so she wriggled down from the bed without a murmur. Bethany climbed up to put the curtain back on its rail, glancing over her shoulder to see what Kitty was up to now. She was trying on Bethany's slippers, which were much too big for her. She couldn't do any harm like that, so Bethany went on rehanging the curtain. When she looked again, Kitty was still dressing up and had got as far as putting on a sweater Bethany had left on a chair. That was safe enough too. Bethany clipped the last curtain hook back into place.

'Ooh!' squeaked Kitty.

Bethany turned sharply, but it was too late.

Kitty had taken Bethany's coat from the cage, meaning to put it on, but had seen Hamilton and forgotten all about dressing up. She was trying to open the cage door as Bethany jumped down and caught her hand.

'No!' Bethany pulled the chubby little fist away from the cage. 'You mustn't touch that!'

'Mouse!' shouted Kitty. 'There's a big mouse in there! Come out, mouse!'

'It's a hamster,' said Bethany, holding firmly on to Kitty's hands as Hamilton glared from behind the bars. 'He's a hamster and he doesn't want to play today.'

Hamilton went straight back to his nest box and pulled the bedding round him. He wanted to make it quite clear to Kitty that he really *didn't* want to play.

'He's making his bed,' said Bethany. 'That means he wants to sleep now, so we have to leave him alone.'

'But I want him!' cried Kitty. 'Get him out!'

'He doesn't want to come out,' said Bethany. 'He's an animal, not a toy. He's gone to hide in his nest box and that means he wants us to leave him alone. We have to be very quiet so he can sleep. Let's see if we can be very quiet, shall we?'

'I'll sing him to sleep,' yelled Kitty with a lunge towards the cage.

'He doesn't like singing,' said Bethany through gritted teeth. He certainly wouldn't have liked Kitty's singing, which was the same as shouting, only louder and off-key.

'I WANT HIM!' yelled Kitty.

'Shall we find the paints?' said Bethany, still holding on to Kitty and trying to change the subject. 'You want to paint a picture, don't you?'

'Not paints!' said Kitty crossly. 'I want to play with *him*!'

'I know, but he doesn't want to play with you,' said Bethany, and picked up her coat from the floor where Kitty had dropped it. 'You were dressing up, weren't you? Here's my coat; shall we see what else we can – Ow!'

The 'Ow!' was because Kitty had kicked Bethany and was struggling hard. Bethany held

on to her as long as she could, but Kitty
fought, wriggled and kicked before escaping to
try to wrench the cage door open again.
Bethany prised her fingers away.

'I DON'T WANNA DRESS UP!'
bellowed Kitty, with a tearful sob in her voice.
'I WANNA DRESS *MOUSIE* UP, all pretty
and frilly and PINK!'

Hamilton had left the safety of his nest when
Bethany said 'Ow!' to see if he could help her.
Hearing Kitty's words, he froze. He was not
going to be 'dressed up'. Not up, not down, not
sideways and definitely not pink. And he was
not called 'Mousie'.

'*No*,' said Bethany firmly. She slipped in
between Kitty and the cage, and stood still.

Kitty tried hitting Bethany, but Bethany
wouldn't move, so instead she tried crying very
loudly. That didn't do any good either and
Hamilton could see exactly why Bethany had

called Kitty a monster. She howled, she screamed, she lay on the floor and kicked, she held her breath until she turned purple. But none of it appeared to make any difference to Bethany. Kitty stopped kicking the floor and banged her head on it instead and when that hurt, she ran howling from the room.

The howling stopped so quickly that Hamilton thought Kitty must have an On/Off switch. Maybe Bethany had run after her and switched her off, or perhaps it worked by remote control, but he was very glad of the silence, and looked out. He couldn't see what was happening on the landing, but he could hear the grunt of the trombone.

He had a feeling that things were about to get even worse. He was right.

chapter 5

Kitty flung open the door to Sam's room and stood quite still in astonishment. She even forgot to howl. Her eyes were wide, her mouth was open and she was staring as if she had seen an angel. Sam, the trombone still at his mouth, stopped in the middle of a grunt. He didn't look at all as if he'd seen an angel. He looked as if he'd seen Kitty.

Kitty drew a deep breath and pointed.

'Trumpet!' she exclaimed with longing.
'I want that trumpet!'

Bethany knelt on the floor beside her and put an arm round her.

'It's very heavy,' she said. 'Much too heavy for you. Listen to . . .' She had meant to say, 'Listen to Sam play', but the noises Sam made didn't sound much like playing yet, so she changed it to, 'Listen to all those lovely sounds Sam makes with it.'

Kitty stepped forward, reaching out to stroke the gleaming brass of the trombone.

'That's called the bell,' said Sam.

'And a pushy thing that goes back and forward,' observed Kitty.

'That bit's called the slide,' explained Sam. 'Do you want to hear it?'

'No,' said Kitty. 'I want to play it.'

'It's very delicate,' said Sam. It didn't look or sound at all delicate, but he didn't like the idea of Kitty touching it. 'And it isn't mine. It belongs to the school, so I mustn't let anyone else –'

Sam wasn't able to finish because at that second he had to leap out of the way as Kitty hurled herself with open arms at the trombone. Bethany held on to her, so she began howling again.

'Don't touch, Kitty,' Bethany said. Kitty screamed, kicked again and was about to start her second tantrum of the afternoon when, over the screams, came Mum's voice.

'Kitty,' she called up the stairs, 'would you like to see a DVD?'

'No DVD!' said Kitty and kicked the wall.

'Oh well, I'll put *Pingu* away, then,' said Mum.

Very soon Kitty stopped screaming. She tried a sob, but Bethany ignored it, so she dried her eyes, sniffed indignantly and ran down the stairs to watch *Pingu*. Sam and Bethany sat down on the landing and sighed with relief.

Hamilton, who had heard it all from his

cage, sighed too. He had had more than enough of Kitty for one day.

'Thank goodness for that,' said Bethany. 'I've got homework to do and I'll do it while it's quiet.'

'And I'm going to do my trombone practice,' said Sam. 'I'll do it in the shed. I think I'll be safe from her in there.'

Bethany went back to her bedroom, shut the door and took Hamilton from the cage. The catch was unusually stiff.

'Poor Hamilton, did you lock yourself in for extra safety?' she said gently, stroking him with one finger. 'That was very sensible of you. Are you all right? I'm sorry about this. Kitty can be really scary, and it's a bit late to take you to Chloe's now. Kitty would see, and want to come with us.'

She let him run from one hand to the other, then gave him the book he had been reading that morning on the Battle of Hastings while she settled down to do her homework. When Hamilton had finished the book – which didn't take long – he ran up and down the curtain a few times for fun, then jumped back into his cage, locking it firmly again. He was already calling it 'kittylocking'. He attended to eating, drinking and washing while Bethany got on with her maths.

Hamilton soon got bored, though. Bethany didn't appear to need any help with her maths today, and Sam's trombone playing still wasn't very good, but it was interesting. He didn't like to bother Bethany, so he unlocked the cage very quietly and slipped out of the room, taking care to stay well away from the sitting room, where he knew Kitty would be watching *Pingu*.

Hamilton had been to the shed before, so he knew where it was. The shed was shut – Sam had locked himself in – but Hamilton was small enough to slip under the door. The trombone wasn't exactly making oompah noises yet, but he didn't mind that. In fact, he could never tell what sound would come out of it next – and now he knew what was making all the different sounds, it was actually great fun.

For a while, everything was calm. Bethany finished her homework, Sam tried to play the trombone, Hamilton listened and Kitty watched another DVD. In the shed, Hamilton and Sam didn't hear the doorbell ring, but Mum did, and went to answer it. Out of curiosity, Bethany went downstairs, and at that moment, the phone rang.

'Hello?' said Mum, picking it up. 'Oh! Nice to hear from you – excuse me a moment!' She put her hand over the phone. 'Bethany, I've got a customer on the phone. Will you answer the door?'

A man stood on the doorstep. He was young, with glasses and blond hair, and his suit looked a bit too big for him. In his left hand he carried a briefcase, and his right hand was held out to shake.

'Good afternoon!' he said. 'My name's Peter and I'm from Pexperts. You asked for a visit.'

chapter 6

The man at the door smiled a little nervously and Bethany took a good look at him as she shook his hand. There was something strangely familiar about him, and she wondered where she might have seen him before. His hair was clearly dyed – she could tell that because it was dark at the roots – so she tried to imagine him with dark hair, but it wasn't easy.

'You left a message on my phone,' he said cheerfully. 'You wanted advice about your hamster?'

'No, I didn't,' said Bethany, 'but let me check with Mum.'

She looked over at Mum, who was just finishing her phone conversation. 'Mum, did you phone somebody for advice about hamsters?'

Mum shook her head, and the look on her face said quite plainly that she was suspicious about this. She came to stand beside Bethany at the door.

'Here's my card,' said the young man, handing over a printed business card. 'And here's my ID and the copy of our leaflet.'

He was really Tim Taverner, of course, but the card said 'Peter Pilkington'. He was becoming very good at fake ID cards. Mum looked at the yellow leaflet.

'Yes, one of these came through the door,' she said. 'I don't think we phoned anyone, though.'

'Unless Dad did,' suggested Bethany. 'He

might have come home at lunchtime.' But she still felt a bit wary of this man.

Tim took out his mobile phone. '"PLS CALL AT 33 TUMBLERS CRESCENT, SPINHILL",' he read from the screen, and held it up to show them the message. Bethany saw her own phone number on the screen.

Oh, Hamilton, thought Bethany. *What have you done?*

'Well, I don't understand it, unless the hamster's learnt to send his own text messages!' said Mum.

Bethany turned deep red and hoped Mum didn't notice. She didn't want anyone to guess how clever Hamilton was, so she'd have to cover up for him.

'Oh, *that* text!' she said. 'Yes, I sent that! Sorry, Mum, I'd forgotten all about it.'

She'd need to have a word with Hamilton about this.

'I wish you'd asked me first, Bethany,' said Mum, but the phone rang again and she went to answer it.

'There's no charge for a first visit,' said Tim. 'Shall I come and meet your hamster?'

Bethany hesitated, wondering what to do next. As she did so, she realized that apart from Mum's voice on the phone, everything had become quiet. It was much too still. The DVD had finished and she couldn't hear a sound from Kitty.

'Excuse me, wait there, please!' she said to the man on the doorstep. Then she banged the door shut in his face and dashed to the kitchen. On an earlier visit, Kitty had flooded the sink while playing with the washing-up liquid, and on another occasion she'd decided to bake a cake and had filled a mixing bowl with flour, milk and tomato sauce before anyone had stopped her. Dreading what she might find, Bethany dashed into the kitchen.

But Kitty wasn't in the kitchen . . . and what could be worse than Kitty in the kitchen?

Kitty upstairs, of course.

Bethany was halfway up the stairs when Kitty appeared on the landing. She was sobbing loudly, but it wasn't the sort of helpless sobbing that means real heartbreak. It was a roar of angry tears because things were not going Kitty's way.

'Your mouse has gone!' howled Kitty.

Bethany rushed past her and into the bedroom. With her heart beating hard and fast and her hand shaking, she looked in the cage and examined the catch on the door. The cage had been opened and neatly closed again and the nest was as tidy as Hamilton had left it.

Bethany took a few deep breaths. If Kitty had opened the cage, she would have left it wide open with the nest spread everywhere. It looked as if Hamilton must have let himself out. Kitty appeared beside her.

'I looked and he'd gone,' she sniffed. 'I just came to see if he was all right.'

'Kitty,' said Bethany, wanting to be quite sure of what had happened, 'did you open the cage? Nobody will be cross. You're not in trouble, only it would be helpful if you tell me the truth. Did you open the cage?'

Kitty sniffed loudly. 'It wouldn't open for me,' she said.

So she tried, thought Bethany. 'How did you know he wasn't hiding in his nest?' she asked.

'Just did,' muttered Kitty. Bethany guessed that she'd tried hitting the cage, but wasn't going to admit it. 'I shouted to him to come out and see me and come and play with me, and he didn't, so I knew he wasn't in his house.'

Bethany looked at the empty cage while she

wondered what to do. Hamilton was capable of hiding somewhere and getting back into his cage again, but if he was outside, there was always the danger that he'd meet with a nasty accident or a cat (which could be the same thing).

Kitty thundered down the stairs. Bethany ran after her to see what she was going to do next – and stop her if necessary.

'Auntie Angela,' yelled Kitty, 'the mousie's gone, Bethany's big mousie's gone away!'

Mum stood at the front door – she had wondered what had happened to the Pexpert man and was surprised to find him still there. She was talking to him as Kitty ran down stairs, threw both arms round her waist and tried to drag her away.

'He's gone, Auntie!' she wailed. 'Bethany's big mousie's gone; come and find him!'

Tim's scientific brain did the following:

Bethany's big mousie = Bethany's hamster

Bethany's hamster = hamster with my microspeck inside it

Hamster + microspeck + escape = THE MICROSPECK COULD BE ANYWHERE AROUND HERE!

Tim tried very hard to keep his hands from shaking with excitement. From his pocket, he took the tracking device that would home in on Hamilton's microspeck. It looked a bit like a mobile phone.

'We'd better find him,' he said.

'What's that?' demanded Kitty, stretching up to see it.

'It's a kind of bleeper to help us find the big mousie,' said Tim. 'What a good thing I had it with me! It's my magical hamster finder.'

'Magic!' said Kitty, and her eyes lit up.

'What is it really?' asked Bethany, who didn't believe in magical hamster finders, but Tim was already gazing at it so carefully that he didn't seem to notice the question. From the front of the device came a very faint flicker and an even fainter bleep. He moved it in different directions.

'We should find him easily enough,' he said. 'Leave it to me. This is what we're trained to do at Pexperts.'

I wish you'd go away, thought Bethany.

Kitty was eyeing the tracking device. 'I want a go!' she demanded, stretching up to take it. Just in time, Tim raised it out of her reach. It had never occurred to him that he would meet with a problem as difficult as Kitty. She stretched up again in another attempt to prise the tracking device from his hand.

I wish you'd both go away, thought Bethany this time. But as long as they *were* here, and Hamilton might be anywhere, Bethany wasn't letting either of them out of her sight.

chapter 7

In the shed, Hamilton was having a simply
wonderful time. He had chatted for a while
with his friend Bobby, who lived in a hutch in
the shed. Bobby was Sam's rabbit, but luckily
Hamilton was fluent in Rabbitspeak.

A pair of Sam's gloves lay beside Bobby's
cage, and so Hamilton had snuggled into one
of them while he and Bobby settled down to
enjoy Sam's trombone practice.

'He's learning to oompah,' explained
Hamilton. 'But he's only just started learning

how to make the right noises. I read about it on the computer.'

'What's a compertooter?' asked Bobby.

'It's a thing with a screen,' said Hamilton, 'like a window. You click all the right things and it's got a mouse, but it isn't a real live mouse. You keep clicking until you find the right bit, and that's how I found the bit about oompah music.'

Bobby tried to make clicking noises with his teeth, but wasn't very successful. He just sounded as if he were muttering to himself.

'The air has to go into the mouthpiece . . .' began Hamilton, then remembered that while he understood the science of valves and air pressure very well, it wouldn't mean anything to the rabbit. 'You have to put a quiet funny noise in at one end, and it goes round all the tubes. That means it's a loud funny noise when it comes out.'

'It's good!' said Bobby, gazing up at Sam in

admiration. 'You never know what it's going to do next!'

'It's supposed to oompah,' said Hamilton, 'but sometimes it ooms and sometimes it pahs because he hasn't got the ooms and the pahs to meet in the middle. Sometimes it isn't quite an oom and a pah, just a poom. It takes a long time before you can do that properly.'

The trombone gave a deep groan.

'Is it hurting?' asked Bobby anxiously.

'No,' said Hamilton. 'It's only playing.'

The more Sam practised with his trombone, the better he got. The noises became louder and stronger, and the slowly drawn-out notes – *pa-a-arp* – *pa-a-arp* – *pa* – *arp* grew closer together. Hamilton could almost dance to this, and Bobby swayed a bit as they listened. When something tingled in his cheek pouch, he hardly noticed it at all.

Sam stopped playing and put the trombone

down in its case. His face was much redder than usual.

'I need a break, Bobby,' he said, and took the rabbit out of his cage to be stroked and talked to. He removed some stale old bits of apple core from the hutch floor, and told Bobby everything he'd been doing at school.

He hadn't noticed Hamilton snuggled down in a glove, and this gave Hamilton the thing he wanted most at that moment. It gave him the chance to explore the trombone, and he couldn't wait. Stopping only to rub at his cheek, which was tingling a lot now, he hopped into the trombone case. Hamilton wondered if he could design and make a very small trombone to play when nobody except Bethany could hear him.

He examined the valves in great detail, patting at them with his paws. Hamilton's microspeck meant that he could measure accurately, and by running from one end of the trombone to the other, he had soon calculated its length. He had even worked out how long the trombone would be if you could unfold it all. Getting more and more curious, and more and more excited to see the place where the sound came out, Hamilton slipped right inside the bell of the trombone to explore.

The tingling in his cheek stopped at once, which surprised him. It puzzled him too. He sat for a moment with his head on one side, thinking hard about this.

Tim Taverner was trying hard to concentrate on the signal from his homing device (which, of course, was the thing making Hamilton's cheek tingle) but with Kitty pulling on his jacket, it was hard for him to concentrate on anything. He had walked slowly and carefully down one side of Bethany's house, back across the front, all the way round twice and back the other way, and finally into the back garden, with Bethany and Kitty following. Bethany stayed close to him because she was curious about what he was doing and didn't trust him. Kitty was there because she was longing to get her hands on the homing device.

'How does it work?' Bethany wanted to know, but Tim pretended not to hear her.

'Hammy, Hammy, Hammy!' shouted Kitty as she raced about the garden. Bethany didn't try to stop her. If Hamilton could hear Kitty – and surely everyone in the street could hear her – he'd keep well out of the way.

'How does it work?' Bethany asked again, more forcefully this time.

'Oh, it's electronic,' said Tim vaguely, scowling as he listened for a signal.

'Yes, but how does it pick up a signal from a hamster?' Bethany persisted.

'Oh, that's too complicated to explain,' said Tim.

'I'm sure *you* could explain it,' said Bethany, hoping that he'd feel flattered.

'It gives out a call sound,' said Tim, who was making it up as he went along and wishing she'd leave him alone.

'Come on, good little hamstery, come to Kitty-witty!' Kitty bellowed, crashing into Tim's legs and making a grab for the tracking device. He was just in time to hold it away from her.

'I can't hear a call sound,' said Bethany. 'I can't hear anything.'

'That's because you're not a hamster,' said Tim. 'It's a signal that only hamsters can hear, but they respond to it.' He looked at the tracking device and felt a tingle of excitement. A pale yellow light was steadily flashing. Very quietly, it beeped.

'He's round here somewhere!' he said.

'Let me have a go!' cried Kitty. He held it away from her, and with a cry of, 'It's my turn!', she hurled herself against him and struggled furiously to climb up him as if he were a tree. 'I want it!' The shout turned into a sob. 'I wa-ha-hant it!'

Bethany dragged her away from him. 'You can't have it, Kitty,' she said. 'It's not a toy.'

'Not fair!' wailed Kitty and kicked her.

'Is it time for you to go in for tea, Kitty?' asked Tim as pleasantly as he could.

Kitty kicked him too.

'Kitty!' said Bethany. 'Go into the house at once!' Kitty aimed another kick, but Bethany dodged. With a cry of rage, Kitty lay on the ground and kicked.

'Sorry about her,' said Bethany. 'She's very naughty.'

'That's quite all right,' said Tim, but he only

said it to be polite. All he wanted was the hamster. In fact, he didn't want the hamster at all, just the tiny microspeck! And what had he ended up with? Kitty.

In the shed, Sam was making very strange faces. Hamilton, who had stopped exploring for a while and come out to see what was happening, understood what Sam was doing. He'd read about it on the computer.

'Is he trying to whistle?' asked Bobby.

'It's called an embouchure,' said Hamilton, who was carefully watching everything Sam did. 'It's no good just blowing down a trombone – you need a special way of doing it. You have to pull faces.' He rubbed his cheek, which was buzzing again.

'Did you find that out on the compotater too?' asked Bobby.

'Pardon?' said Hamilton, who was still

watching Sam's strange faces in fascination.
'Oh, yes. On the Internet.'

The only net Bobby knew about was the
wire netting on the front of his hutch and his
garden run. He wondered whether the Internet
was anything like wire netting and whether
there was any Internet lying around in the
shed.

As Bobby thought this over, Hamilton ran to
the trombone and climbed inside it again. He
liked it in there – his cheek didn't buzz when
he was in the trombone. Besides, he hadn't
finished exploring.

'No, Kitty,' said Bethany very firmly. 'That is a
very important piece of equipment, and it
belongs to Mister Pexperts. You're not to touch
it.' She didn't like Mr Pexperts at all, but she
was trying to make Kitty behave.

Kitty let out a screech that sent the crows

flying from the trees as she hung off Tim Taverner's jacket. The scream hadn't got her what she wanted, so she tried holding her breath instead, but Tim didn't seem to notice that she was turning scarlet. He was struggling to prise her fingers from his jacket while keeping the tracking device out of her reach with his other hand. The flashing light was stronger and clearer now, and the beep louder. He turned in all directions, trying to find where the signal was strongest, with Kitty still hanging on.

Tim found that the light and the beep were at their clearest when he faced the shed at the bottom of the garden. He marched purposefully towards it, trying to pretend that Kitty wasn't there.

'I'm pretty certain he's in that shed,' he announced. 'Looks like the perfect hiding place for a hamster!'

And you're not getting your hands on him, thought Bethany, staying close beside him and a step ahead. She didn't trust him one little bit.

Kitty lost her grip on Tim, fell over, lay on the grass and howled, but when she realized that nobody was taking any notice, she got up and ran after them.

'There's a bunny rabbit in there,' she said.

'Is there?' asked Tim hopefully. This was encouraging. 'A bunny rabbit?' Where there was a rabbit, there would be rabbit food, and where there was rabbit food, there might well be a hamster. The tracking device certainly thought the hamster was in there.

'I'll show you the bunny rabbit,' said Kitty, pulling on Tim's hand. 'It's in here.'

By this time, Tim was anxious to get Kitty out of the way, and not just because she was by far the most irritating child he'd ever met. He didn't want Kitty running into the garden shed yelling 'Hamster!' or 'Bunny rabbit!' at the top of her voice and scaring everything away.

'Don't you think you should go back to your mummy now?' he suggested.

Kitty pouted. 'My mummy's gone!' she cried dramatically.

'Oh!' said Tim. He hadn't expected this and felt very uncomfortable.

'Kitty's my cousin,' said Bethany. 'She doesn't live here, we're just looking after her until her mum comes to collect her. Kitty, would you like to go and see what Auntie Angela's doing?'

Bethany needed to make sure that Kitty was out of the way so that she might get to Hamilton before her cousin or this man did. Normally, mentioning Auntie Angela might have worked, but Kitty was too excited to listen and too determined to get hold of the tracking device, which was now beeping steadily.

Tim moved towards the shed. The bleep was louder now, and more frequent. The light flashed clearly. Bethany saw it and bit her lip. She didn't like not knowing where Hamilton was, but the idea of this stranger or Kitty finding him was far worse. What was Mr Pexperts really up to? *Run, Hamilton,* she thought. *Run and keep running, and stay out of the way.*

They were at the shed door. As Tim put out his hand to open it, the bleep stopped as abruptly as if it had been switched off.

'We've lost him!' said Tim. 'Now where's he gone?'

'BUNNY RABBIT!' bellowed Kitty.

Hamilton, thought Bethany. *Where are you?*

chapter 8

Hamilton sat in the bell of the trombone, the sturdy metal stopping Tim Taverner's tracking device from finding him. The device could track through many things, but not through a trombone. As long as Hamilton was in there, the signal couldn't find him.

Then a lot of things happened all at once.

Sam picked up the trombone and held it to his lips. He decided it was time to find out if he'd got his embouchure right.

Kitty threw open the door. 'Hello, bunny-

bunny-bunny!' she shouted. 'I've come to play!'

She darted to the rabbit hutch as Sam drew in the deepest breath he could and blew hard into the trombone. Out from the bell came a loud and terrifying noise – and Hamilton.

Tim hurled himself forward in an effort to catch the hamster. Bethany dashed in front of him, then he tripped over her and landed on Kitty, who screamed and hit him. She kept on hitting him as he struggled to get up again – and the more he struggled, the more she pounded him with her fists. Hamilton had sailed on past them and landed on Bethany's shoulder as she scrambled to her feet. He ran down her arm and, with her help, into the sleeve of her sweater, where he hid. Bethany looked for the tracking device, but it had fallen out of Tim's hand as he fell and wasn't making any sound at all. In the meantime, Tim was still trying to get up and Kitty was still hitting him.

'Kitty! Stop it at once!' said Bethany. 'I'm very sorry, Mister Pexperts,' she added, but had to bite her lip to keep from laughing.

'Oh, Kitty,' said Sam wearily, and left the trombone in its case while he helped Bethany to drag Kitty away from Tim. Kitty had forgotten all about rabbits and hamsters by now – she'd even forgotten why she was so cross, but she went on hitting Tim, and fought against Sam and Bethany as they took an arm each and heaved her away.

'No!' she screamed. 'No, no, no, let me go, naughty Bethany, naughty Sam! I don't like you any more, let me go! You smell!'

She twisted, kicked, struggled and howled, but Bethany and Sam held on to her. Shaking, bedraggled and astonished, Tim staggered to his feet. His clothes were not only crumpled, but also dirty from the shed floor, his shoes were badly scuffed, and his keys, his phone and several screwdrivers had fallen out of his pockets. He stuffed them back in again and adjusted his glasses. Sam, who had no idea who this man was, picked up the tracking device and rubbed it on his sleeve.

'I don't know what it is, but I think it's broken,' he said, handing it back to Tim.

'I can mend it,' muttered Tim with grim determination. Bethany tried to dust him down, but he wrenched himself away from her.

'I'm really very sorry about all this,' said Bethany, and she meant it. She was truly very concerned about him. 'Kitty, what have you got to say to Mister Pexperts?'

'You smell,' said Kitty. She folded her arms, tilted her chin down and her shoulders up, and scowled.

'Kitty, that's very rude,' said Sam, so she kicked him.

'Kitty!' It was Mum's voice, and to Bethany and Sam at that moment it was the best sound in the whole world. She was standing in the shed doorway, and was too concerned about a very messy Kitty kicking Sam to worry about the Pexpert man.

'That's not very nice, is it, Kitty?' she said. 'Don't kick Sam. And look at the state of your clothes; have you been rolling around on the floor? Now, you come with me because your mum's here to take you home.'

For a moment, Kitty looked as if she might argue, but there was no more fun to be had. She couldn't kick anyone now that her Auntie Angela was there, and if she screamed she'd just be tucked under Auntie Angela's arm and carried inside. She took her aunt's hand and walked meekly back to the house.

By this time, Tim had decided that enough was enough. The tracking device had been

smashed on the shed floor and was useless.
He had no hope of finding the hamster now –
it was nowhere to be seen and must have run
away from the shed in all the chaos. His knees
were grazed, he was bruised from Kitty's
kicks and punches, and all he wanted was
to get away from this house as quickly as
possible. He did wonder about telling the
police that he'd been assaulted, but then they'd
find out that he was using a false name and
pretending to be something he wasn't. Besides,
he couldn't very well say he'd been beaten up
by a little girl.

Bethany and Sam walked with him as far as
the car and waved goodbye.

'Who was that?' asked Sam.

'Just some sort of pet man,' said Bethany.

'You can't keep men as pets,' said Sam, and
seemed to find this extremely funny. 'Bethany
wants a pet man!'

'Shut up and don't be stupid,' said Bethany. 'I mean, a man who knows about pets. He's supposed to be an expert on hamsters.'

'What did he say about Hamilton?' asked Sam.

'He couldn't even find him,' said Bethany, and then it all seemed very funny to her too.

While Kitty was in the kitchen with Auntie Sally and Bethany's mum, Bethany went quietly back up to her room. She reached into her sleeve for Hamilton and stroked him.

'It's all right now, Hamilton,' she said. 'She's going home. And that strange man's gone. I'm sorry you haven't had a very nice afternoon.'

Hamilton looked hard at his cage, then at Bethany, then – in case she hadn't understood – back at his cage again.

'You want to go for a sleep?' she said. 'Yes, of course.' She put him back into his cage and fastened the door. He closed it extra firmly from the inside, as he knew that Kitty was still somewhere in the house.

He had learnt today about trombones and Monstrous Kitties, and they were both very tiring. He rearranged the nest, curled up in it and fell asleep.

chapter 9

In the kitchen, Kitty sat quietly on her
mother's lap while Bethany's mum made coffee
and handed Kitty a glass of orange juice. Kitty
made gurgling noises into it.

'Don't do that, darling,' said her mum.
'What have you been doing while I was away?
Have you been a good girl?'

'I've been as good as gold,' said Kitty,
snuggling against her mum and kicking her
legs contentedly. 'I went to Bethany's room
and played, and Bethany's got a big fluffy

mouse and a funny man came with a magic box.'

'What man, darling?' asked her mum.

'She means the pet consultant,' said Mum. 'He's supposed to be a specialist on rodents or something.'

'Yes,' said Kitty firmly. 'Oh dense or somethings.'

'You mean ro – dents,' said Auntie Sally. 'That's the word for little animals with sharp teeth who gnaw things. Can you say "rodents"?'

'Dense,' repeated Kitty decisively. 'Dense. He was the Dense Man and he had little sharp teeth. He went all round the garden with the magic box.' A daydreamy look came into her face. The more she thought about it, the more her imagination went to work on the story. 'He had a magic box with a fairy light and it made a sound like Tinkerbell to make the fairies come. And we went into the shed and it was all full of fairies all flying about and Sam was playing a great big shiny trumpet and the big furry mouse jumped out of the trumpet and it had wings and it flew over our heads with the fairies, and I waved my magic wand.'

Her mother hugged her tightly. 'You have the most wonderful imagination, darling!' she said.

'I know.' Kitty hugged her mum back before wriggling off her lap and skipping away to watch cartoons. But before she could reach the television, she heard the bathroom door open and shut. Kitty gasped in delight. This meant that Bethany was finally out of the way and Kitty could get her hands on Hamilton!

She ran up to Bethany's room to see if the Giant Fluffy Mouse was in his cage. Ever so quietly, Kitty pushed open the door of Bethany's room and tiptoed in.

Back in his cage, Hamilton had woken up

and was practising his embouchure – perhaps
he could make noises down a trombone too. It
would be difficult, but he might find some
useful materials – silver foil, maybe, and the
things Bethany put in her hair – that he could
make into a hamster-sized trombone, or
something like one. It would be fun to try.

He screwed up his mouth and pushed out
his teeth. That was better, and he pretended
to hold a trombone in his paws, pushing the
slide in and out. He was concentrating so
hard that he didn't notice Kitty creeping
softly into the room.

Kitty's hand was on the catch. She knew this
cage wasn't easy to open, but a good wrench
should do it.

She had been about to say, 'Come on,
mousie, come to Kitty,' but she didn't. When
she looked at Hamilton, she was too frightened
to say anything at all.

Bethany's Giant Fluffy Mouse was pulling faces – horrible, scary faces! It had bared its teeth and stretched out its mouth and was waving its paws back and forth in the air like angry fists! It wanted to eat her! Kitty's mouth opened wide in horror.

Hamilton felt he was doing rather well with his embouchure, but it was hard work. To relax his mouth muscles, he chewed at the bars of his cage.

Seeing this obvious attempt by the scary Giant Fluffy Mouse to chew his way out of the cage before eating her, Kitty backed away towards the door. She had had enough. When Bethany returned from the bathroom, Kitty turned and fled back down the stairs.

'Hamilton!' cried Bethany, running over to his cage to check that he was OK, 'has Kitty been bothering you?'

Hamilton looked round. Kitty? He shook his

head. He hadn't even seen the Monstrous Kitty.

'Good,' said Bethany. She sat down and picked up her phone. 'Hamilton, I wonder why that pet man came today. He said somebody had phoned him and asked him to visit. It wasn't me.'

Hamilton put his head on one side and looked innocent.

'Hamilton,' said Bethany, opening the cage and taking him out, 'I'm not going to be cross. I just want to know – did you send for the pet man?'

Hamilton nodded sadly. He already wished he hadn't done it. That pet man had spoilt a very happy tromboning session.

'Then, Hamilton,' said Bethany, 'you must never send messages to people you don't know. Especially, you mustn't invite them here. For all you know, they might not be very nice people. Do you understand?'

79

Hamilton nodded eagerly. He hadn't liked the pet man.

'In fact,' said Bethany, 'don't text anyone, ever, except me. And don't ever send an email. We can't let people know that you're such a clever hamster, can we?'

Hamilton thought about this. He liked texting, but he could see Bethany's point. He twitched his nose and puckered his mouth to show that he wasn't pleased, but he didn't try to argue.

Bethany was just filling up his food bowl and water bottle when Mum looked round the door.

'Kitty and Auntie Sally are going home now,' she said. 'Do you want to say goodbye? Kitty doesn't want to come up here. I can't understand why.'

Kitty was strangely quiet as they left the house. There wasn't a word about the giant mouse, or the rabbit, or the man with the magic box. She trotted to the car holding her mum's hand tightly.

'Thank goodness for that,' said Sam as the car door slammed shut.

'Sam!' said Mum. 'I know she's hard work, but she's your cousin.'

'Bethany,' said Sam as they went back upstairs. 'Was that really your hamster in my trombone?'

Bethany did wonder for a moment whether she should pretend to have no idea what Sam was talking about. But that wouldn't work. She had to be as truthful as possible.

'Yes, it was,' she said. 'I wish I knew how he got in there. It could have been dangerous.'

'It was probably Kitty's fault,' said Sam. 'Is Hammy all right?'

They went into Bethany's room together. For Hamilton, it had been a tiring day and he hadn't slept much. After supper and a drink, he had made his nest comfortable and settled down to go back to sleep.

'All he ever does is eat and sleep,' said Sam, and went back to his trombone.

chapter 10

At the university, Tim limped into the laboratory and kicked the waste-paper basket because he needed to kick something. It fell over, spilling paper and apple cores across the floor. He kicked the desk too, which hurt his toes. Then he flopped down heavily in his swivel chair and inspected his trousers, which had got very dirty when he fell. He supposed they'd be all right if the dry cleaners could get the marks out.

He wouldn't have minded getting dirty, or

even being attacked by the terrible Kitty – he wouldn't even have minded the bruises – if only he'd got hold of the hamster and the microspeck. He put his head in his hands – he had been so close, *so* close to getting hold of that hamster and getting the microspeck back.

He began to wonder if he'd imagined it all. Surely the hamster couldn't really have jumped out of a trombone? Why was the boy playing the trombone in the shed? Tim was already seeing that hamster in his dreams. Maybe he was beginning to see it when he was awake too, even if it wasn't there. But he wasn't imagining the bruises.

Somebody knocked at the door and he jumped – but it was only Mary the cleaner, standing at the door with her vacuum cleaner and her box of dusters and polish.

'Doctor Taverner?' she said. She had been watching him for a few minutes now and was worried. At first she hadn't been quite sure if it really was Dr Taverner at all because he had dyed his hair blond, but, yes, it was definitely him. The poor man had just buried his head in his hands as if he needed to hold it on. Poor Dr Taverner – he must have been working too hard again – or maybe he just wished he hadn't had his hair done.

'Is it all right to do your cleaning now, Doctor Taverner?' she asked. 'And what about a cup of tea?'

Without waiting for an answer, she put the kettle on. When she brought the tea, Tim was swivelling gently from side to side in his chair.

'You've changed your hair colour, Doctor Taverner,' she said.

'What?' Tim had forgotten about the blond dye. 'Oh – oh, yes.'

'It looks very nice,' she said. It didn't, but she wanted to make him feel better. For the first time, she noticed how grubby he was. 'Look at the state of you!' she exclaimed. 'Did you fall off your bicycle?'

'There was a shed,' said Tim slowly and thoughtfully as he tried to make sense of all that had happened. 'And a small boy with a trombone.'

'I see,' said Mary. Poor Dr Taverner seemed to be very confused. Perhaps he'd fallen asleep and had a nightmare.

'Then the hamster jumped out,' he said.

'What hamster?' she asked.

'The hamster,' he said a bit impatiently. 'The one I have to catch. It was in there.'

'In the shed?' said Mary. 'In a cage?'

'No, in the trombone,' said Tim.

Mary stood up, looking stern. 'There's no need to be sarcastic,' she said. 'I've got work to do.'

'I'm not!' cried Tim. 'The hamster! Really

and honestly, Mary! It just flew out of the
trombone!'

Mary sat down again. 'Flew?' she repeated.

It began to dawn upon Tim that this must
sound even more ridiculous to Mary than it
had been at the time.

'I mean, jumped,' said Tim.

'So,' said Mary, 'let me see if I've understood
this. There was a boy in a shed, and he was
practising his trombone. My son used to play
the trombone when he was at school. You get
some rude noises out of it when you're first
learning, and it frightened the cat. I wish we'd
had a garden shed – I'm sure I would have sent
him to practise in it. That's quite reasonable so
far, Doctor Taverner, nothing to be upset
about. And as for the hamster, maybe it was
just a little fieldmouse.'

'No, it was definitely that hamster,' said
Tim. 'It set off the bleep.'

Mary decided not to ask any more questions. The poor man had obviously been working far too hard. As she closed the door, she shook her head. A hamster in a trombone? Whatever next!

'Goodnight, Hamilton, sleep tight,' said Bethany as she went to bed. 'And thanks for settling Kitty down. I don't know how you did it, but she was as good as gold when she came downstairs.'

In the cosy warmth of his nest box, Hamilton had already fallen asleep, curled up tightly. It wasn't time yet for his nightly run on the wheel. His paws twitched. In his dreams he was leaping, dancing and waltzing through the air, all to the oompah-oompah of a band of trombones.

It all started with a Scarecrow.

Puffin is seventy years old.

Sounds ancient, doesn't it? But Puffin has never been
so lively. We're always on the lookout for the next big
idea, which is how it began all those years ago.

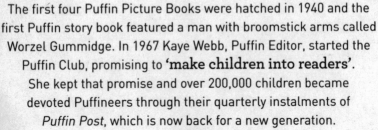

Penguin Books was a big idea from the mind of
a man called Allen Lane, who in 1935 invented
the quality paperback and changed the world.

**And from great Penguins, great Puffins grew,
changing the face of children's books forever.**

The first four Puffin Picture Books were hatched in 1940 and the
first Puffin story book featured a man with broomstick arms called
Worzel Gummidge. In 1967 Kaye Webb, Puffin Editor, started the
Puffin Club, promising to **'make children into readers'**.
She kept that promise and over 200,000 children became
devoted Puffineers through their quarterly instalments of
Puffin Post, which is now back for a new generation.

Many years from now, we hope you'll look back and
remember Puffin with a smile. **No matter what your age
or what you're into, there's a Puffin for everyone.**
The possibilities are endless, but one thing is for sure:
whether it's a picture book or a paperback, a sticker book
or a hardback, **if it's got that little Puffin
on it – it's bound to be good.**